Snoring Shanmugam

story Radhika Chadha

pictures Priya Kuriyan

Tulika

S n o r t.

Hutoxi the horse was upset.
She tossed her mane and snorted
an angry little snort.
Hutoxi was upset with
Shanmugam the lion.

"He's so lazy!" she said. "Is that how the king of the jungle should be?"

S n o r t.

"Don't be upset," Amma the elephant told Hutoxi. "It is good that we have a gentle lion as king. What if we had a cruel king instead?"

"But *look* at him," said Hutoxi.

"All day he does just two things.

He eats.

And he sleeps."

All the animals looked at Shanmugam.

Shanmugam was asleep. As usual.

Shanmugam slept for twenty hours a day.

The rest of the time he ate.

And the more he ate, the longer he slept.

But did Hutoxi say that Shanmugam did just two things all day? No, he did three things. He ate. He slept. And he snored. He lay on his back and he snored. What a snore he had! It went something like this — **khorhrhrh**.......... phsheew..........

khorhrhrh.....

From far away, all that could be heard was the
loud . . . **khorhrhrh**..........
But from up close could be heard the soft,
hissing . . . phsheew..........
When Shanmugam took a deep breath, his tummy
became round . . . **khorhrhrh**..........
And when Shanmugam let out his breath, his
tummy became flat . . . phsheew..........

phsheew.......

Mannu the monkey had great fun sitting on
Shanmugam's tummy.
Khorhrhrh.......... and Mannu went up, up, up, up, up.
Phsheew........... and Mannu came down, down, down.
"Come along for the joyride!" Mannu called out to
Bahadur the baby elephant.

But Bahadur didn't like the idea of sitting
on Shanmugam's tummy.
"Oh, someone stop him snoring," snorted Hutoxi.

There was a simple way to makc him stop.
Shanmugam only snored when he slept on his back.
So Amma used her strong trunk to gently roll him
onto his side and he stopped snoring!
It was quiet once more.
Mannu the monkey swung back to his tree.
Ritu the rabbit scurried off to her hole.
Chandu the crocodile crawled back to the river.
Hutoxi the horse went off with Bahadur and Amma.

That day, the jungle was quiet and peaceful.
Shanmugam slept silently, on his side.
At the edge of the jungle, Kamalnayan the camel
was coming in from the desert.
Suddenly he heard a scary sound.
It was the roar of a new lion.
A lean, mean, brawny, tawny lion . . .

. . . Gabbar Singh!

Gabbar Singh was looking for a jungle
to make his home.

"This looks like a good spot," he said.

"I see no lion pug marks around.

So there must be no other lion in this jungle.

And I smell food!"

Gabbar Singh sniffed and smiled a nasty smile.

"I smell horse.

I smell rabbit.

I smell piglets.

I smell monkey.

I smell baby elephant.

And, mmmmm.... is that camel I smell?"

Kamalnayan hurried over to give his friends
the bad news.

"I'm so scared," squeaked Ritu the rabbit.

"Little ones, stay close to me," snuffled Paytu
the pig, collecting her piglets around her.

"See, what a useless king we have!" snorted Hutoxi.
Amma looked worried.

"As long as we have Shanmugam, we can roam
free in the jungle," she said.

"But if that nasty Gabbar Singh comes we will
have a horrible time."

They all went to Shanmugam.

"Wake up, Shanmugam, wake up!" shrieked Mannu.

But Shanmugam was lying on his side, fast asleep.

"Oh, what use is it even if he wakes up!" snorted Hutoxi.

"If that fellow sees what a soft, gentle lion king we have,
he will throw Shanmugam out of the jungle."

Just then Bahadur had an idea.

He whispered it to Amma.

Amma smiled.

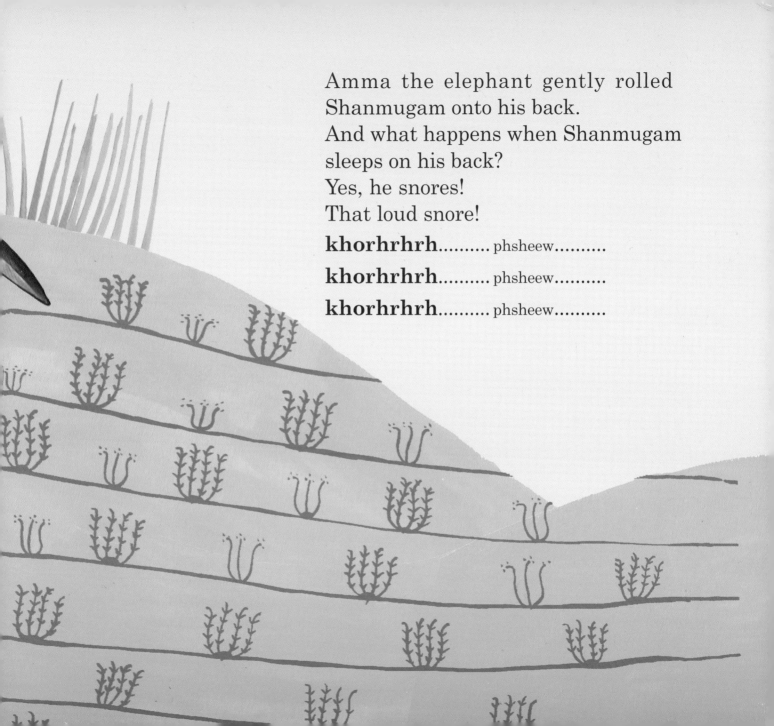

Amma the elephant gently rolled
Shanmugam onto his back.
And what happens when Shanmugam
sleeps on his back?
Yes, he snores!
That loud snore!

khorhrhrh.......... phsheew..........
khorhrhrh.......... phsheew..........
khorhrhrh.......... phsheew..........

Now from where Gabbar Singh was standing he
couldn't hear the soft, hissing phsheew..........
He could only hear the loud **khorhrhrh**..........
Gabbar Singh stopped and looked around.

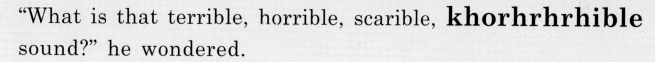

"What is that terrible, horrible, scarible, **khorhrhrhible**
sound?" he wondered.

"I've never heard a roar like that before!
There must be a really big, strong lion in this jungle.
I had better slink away before he sees me."

Gabbar Singh turned and hurried out of the jungle and was
never seen there again.

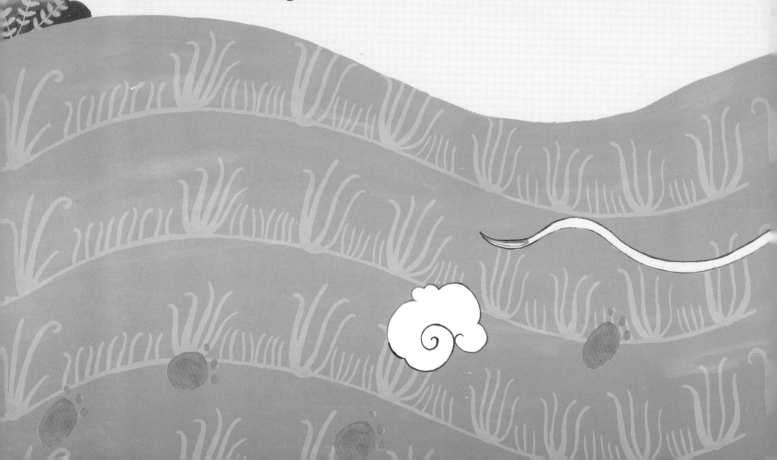

The animals cheered.

"What a clever little elephant you are!" they told Bahadur.

The noise woke up Shanmugam.

He yawned and stretched.

He was surprised to see all the animals around him.

"What's the matter?" he asked.

"Did my snoring trouble you?"

"Not at all," they replied.

"Snore away, Shanmugam!"

For my son Raghav, who helped me bring the sounds alive in words. • R. C.

Other titles in this bestselling series:

(available in English, Hindi, Tamil, Malayalam, Kannada, Telugu, Marathi, Gujarati, Bengali)

I'm So Sleepy
Colour-Colour Kamini
Mallipoo, Where Are You?
Yes, Hutoxi!

Snoring Shanmugam (English)

ISBN 978-81-8146-190-2
© *text* Radhika Chadha
© *illustrations* Priya Kuriyan
First published in India, 2006
Reprinted in 2009, 2011, 2012, 2014, 2017

Published by
Tulika Publishers, 24/1 Ganapathy Colony Third Street, Teynampet, Chennai 600 018, India
email tulikabooks@vsnl.com *website* www.tulikabooks.com

Printed and bound by
Abi Printers, 6A, P. V. Vaithyalingam Road, Old Pallavaram, Chennai 600 117